Danny Paints a Picture

written and photographed
by
Mia Coulton

Dad was painting a picture.

Look at Dad's picture.

It is a picture of Danny.

Danny wanted
to paint a picture, too.

He got paint, a paint brush,
water and paper.

paint

paint brush

water

paper

He put the paint brush
in his mouth.

He began to paint
a picture.

First he put blue paint
on the paper.

Next he put red paint
on the paper.

Then he put brown and green paint on the paper.

Danny looked at his picture.
He wanted Dad to come and
look at his picture.

Dad came to look at
Danny's picture.

He turned it this way
and that way.

"Oh my," said Dad.
"It must be a picture of me!"